Come, Meet NOAH

Come, Meet NOAH

The Story of Genesis 5-11

Kitty Anna Griffiths

ZONDERVAN
PUBLISHING HOUSE

OF THE ZONDERVAN CORPORATION | GRAND RAPIDS, MICHIGAN 49506

Other books in the COME, MEET series:

> Adam and Eve
> Noah
> Abraham, the Pioneer
> Abraham, God's Friend
> Isaac
> Jacob, the Grabbing Twin
> Jacob, God's Prince
> Joseph, God's Dreamer
> Joseph, the Grand Vizier
> Ruth
> Jesus, the Baby
> Jesus, the Boy

All the above books are on cassette, as are many other stories, all told by the author with music and sound effects. They are obtainable from "A Visit with Mrs. G.," Box 179, Station J, Toronto, Ontario, Canada.

Come, Meet Noah
© 1975, 1977 by Kitty Anna Griffiths
First Zondervan edition — 1977

Second printing 1979

Library of Congress Cataloging in Publication Data

Griffiths, Kitty Anna.
  Come, meet Noah.

  (Come, meet series)
  SUMMARY: A retelling of the Old Testament story about the survival of Noah, his family, and animals during forty days and nights of rain.
  1. Noah — Juvenile literature. 2. Bible. O.T. — Biography — Juvenile literature. [1. Noah's ark. 2. Bible stories — O. T.] I. Willy. II. Title.
BS580.N6G74 1976   222'.11'09505   76-48619

ISBN 0-310-25181-8

Printed in the United States of America

To Jennifer Jane
with love

God had made a beautiful world, and He had put beautiful people in it. But His archenemy, Satan, had done a thorough job of spoiling it.

Satan had wormed his way in and undermined God's authority. Adam and Eve had listened to Satan and disobeyed God – and their relationship with God was ruined. No more friendly visits with their Creator. Now it was exile and sacrifice. And those two beautiful people – God's masterpieces – became the parents of the first murderer.

Things went from bad to worse till they were hopeless. Altogether hopeless.

But God had a rescue plan for those who would listen. That is what this book is about. It's exciting!

All these stories were first told on radio on the author's internationally popular radio story program, "A Visit With Mrs. G."

Contents

1. Operation Rescue 7
2. Countdown 17
3. Water, Water Everywhere.................. 31
4. Off to a New Start 41
5. Any Day Now! 47
6. Noah's "Accident"........................ 53
7. Building Without a Permit.................. 66

1

Operation Rescue

"I simply can't take any more of this. I've had enough!"

And you'll never guess who was speaking. It was God!

No!

Yes.

"I can't take any more," God said. "I've had enough."

And when God's had enough, somebody's had it!

Now it isn't any wonder that God had had enough, is it? Something had to happen. Just think back.

God had made a lovely world, absolutely beautiful. He'd put wonderful people into that world — Adam and Eve. You remember.

Then there was that awful day when Eve disobeyed God. She listened to Satan instead.

And Eve got Adam to listen to her. And the fat was in the fire. God was terribly sad about it, but He had to turn them out of Eden.

Then there was Cain, their first son. That was another terrible story. He killed his brother Abel, you remember. And he had to be banished.

Then there was a bright spot: Seth was born. He grew up to be a very good man. In fact, he was the person whom God was going to use to get His great plan going. And Seth did. Got people worshiping God, did Seth.

But, would you believe it, Seth's family — his children, grandchildren, and great-grandchildren — went wrong. The good ones in Seth's family were few and far between.

There was Enoch: God took him to heaven without dying.

Then there was Methuselah: he lived to a very great age — 969, the oldest person ever.

And there was Noah. (Watch Noah! We're coming back to Noah.)

Well, Seth's family went wrong. Mind you, other families went wrong, too. It was terrible. It all came from their turning their backs on God and listening to Satan.

They listened so much and got so friendly with Satan and his demons that these wicked spirits got into people's marriages.

"There's no mending this," God said. "I wish I'd never made man at all. Their immoral, filthy, cruel behavior is making a foul smell, a stink, right up here to heaven. I'll have to wipe them out — wash all the vile filth away."

But then God said, "One more chance. I won't be in a hurry; I'll give them another chance. I'll send them a preacher who'll do a demonstration as well.

"Where's Noah — my friend, Noah?"

Now we read in the Bible that Noah was a good man. God was very fond of Noah — talked with him, trusted him. Noah walked with God. Good men had been scarce for a long time, as I told you; only one just here and there now for years. Looking for a good man was like looking for a needle in a haystack.

"Noah!" God called.

"Oh, Noah, things are very bad and getting worse. It can't go on. I must clean away — wipe out — all this filth and cruelty and corruption.

"Listen, Noah, to what I have to tell you. Don't get frightened. You are my righteous servant, my friend. You don't have anything to worry about. You are going to preach, Noah — a long sermon."

"Oh, Lord, I'm not a — "

"It's going to be a sermon illustrated by a large visual aid. You'll have to talk some, but it will come naturally out of the visual aid.

"Tell the people:

"One, I am sick and tired of their behavior; it can't go on. (They'll laugh. Expect it.)

"Two, I'm sending a flood, a deluge — very much rain. The situation will be rather like it was before I divided the waters at Creation — water everywhere, like one vast ocean. No earth to be seen. No trees. Nothing but water and your ark — oh, I'll tell you about the ark in a minute. (They'll laugh more. They'll mock.)

"Three, if they repent, there'll be a place in the ark for them. (They'll laugh you to scorn.)

"Now for the ark, the big visual aid: it's a big boat for your safety when the judgment — the deluge — falls.

"You will go into it with your family and two of every creature living on the earth. A male and a female of every animal, every bird, every insect, every reptile that lives will come into the ark with you, so that life will go on afterwards. There'll be seven of some kinds. (But more of that later. I'll give you details of who's to go in, what's to go in, later on.)

"Whoever, whatever, goes into the ark will be absolutely safe from the judgment waters. The ark will be completely waterproof. You are engaged in a great rescue operation, Noah."

"What's the shape and size of the ark to be, Lord?"

"Ah, yes. Here are the plans, Noah. Blueprints. All here. And ask Me any questions any time. In the meantime, build! People will stand around and ask questions. Answer them. That will be you preaching."

The plans said to use gopher wood for building because it was hard and unrottable. There was to be tar for waterproofing.

Size: (oh, my!) 300 cubits — 450 feet long; 50 cubits — 75 feet wide; 30 cubits — 45 feet high. Oh, some boat! Three stories.

Well, Noah got started. He hired helpers. (People will usually work for money even if they're not sold on the project.)

As the great planks of gopher wood were being cut and assembled into a simply colossal boat, people asked questions all right: "What?" — "Why?" — "How on earth?" —

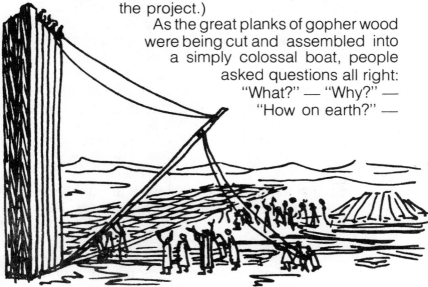

11

"Where?" —
"When?" —
"How long?"

"God is going to send a great flood," Noah said.
"He's going to punish — wipe out — all the cruelty and
filthy living that's going on. The rivers will overflow. The
oceans will spread all over the dry land. And every
living thing on the earth will die. Only what is safely in
the ark will live. Why don't you repent? There'll be room
in the ark for you."

"Oh, I think I'd like my name put down for a place in
your ark, Noah, when the time comes," I can hear
someone say. "Oh, thanks for telling us, Noah."

"Ha! ha! ha! Listen to that! You're as crazy as he is.
Who'd ever believe such nonsense?" comes a mocking
voice.

"No, cross me off for now. I'll think about it later."

Noah took a lot of ridicule, you may be sure. But he
kept at it.

The ark had been under construction for eighteen

years when Noah had a little son. Noah was the very proudest poppa and Mrs. Noah the very proudest mama. They called the baby Shem and thanked God for him.

"Now that crazy old Noah has got a little boy, maybe he'll stop his crazy hobby. Boat-building on dry land! Ha! ha! ha!"

"Let's hope, for goodness' sake, that he won't involve the poor kid in his stupid idiotic notions." People were rude.

While Shem was quite a little fellow, Mr. and Mrs. Noah had another son, a brother for Shem. They called him Ham. And not too long afterwards, another baby boy. They called him Japheth. Shem, Ham, and Japheth were Noah's three sons.

In no time at all, those little boys could be seen helping their dad in one way and another — and with the building. (Would you believe it, Noah was still building that great ark!)

"Just look at that! Noah brainwashing his poor kids into that! It's okay if he wants to be a fool himself, but why involve his kids?"

But the boys spoke up for themselves: "We have our own faith in God, not just father's, thank you."

People thought Noah was mad all right.

"Noah, just look at you. Here you are miles from the ocean, miles from a river, miles from any decent-sized lake. Besides, what river could take a boat that size? The money, the time, the work you've put into that stupid thing!"

"The water will be right here under your very feet, God says," said Noah. "Why won't you listen and repent?"

"Oh, get away! This invisible God of yours — you say He spoke to you? Speaks to you? Ha! Ha! We don't believe a word of it."

Poor Noah! They wouldn't listen. But he kept at it, and the ark grew and grew. It could be seen for miles around.

Time passed. . . .

Shem, Ham, and Japheth were men now. They had married and had chosen their wives carefully — nice girls who believed in "the ark project" and backed it wholeheartedly, 100 percent. They'd have to, wouldn't they? I never did catch their names, but I'm told that Mrs. Shem, Mrs. Ham, and Mrs. Japheth were really nice girls.

Yes, Noah's sons were married, but they had no children yet. Now you and I would say that Noah's sons were getting on in years. In fact, they were nearly a hundred years old. Shem was ninety-eight. But you'll remember that in those days people lived to a great age without getting what we today call "old."

Anyway, all their lives Shem, Ham, and Japheth had helped their father, Noah, to build the ark.

Noah had been at it 120 years!

At last, the job was done. The ark was *finished!*
Oh, you should see what they've been doing all these years. It's magnificent. Look at it! A real landmark, though it's a boat! Wow! It's high and long and wide! I'm going to have a closer look. Coming?

Wait a minute. There's an old man walking beside it — I guess that's Noah. Maybe I can catch him.

"Noah!"

"Yes."

"Oh, I want to ask you some questions about the ark. How — ?"

"Come again!" he shouts. "I'm too busy just now to answer any questions. I'll tell you what you want to know when you come next time."

16

2

Countdown

"Mr. Noah!"

"Where did you come from?"

"Christian Era two-zero-zero-zero [C.E. 2000]," I said.

"Oh, I'm sorry I didn't have time to talk when you came the other day. There was something I simply had to see to. I can't remember what it was now. But it's a good thing you didn't wait too long before coming back. Time's running out fast." Noah's eyes flashed. He had a clever, alert face.

"Time's running out?" I said.

"Yes," he said, "that's what it's all about — my boat. I don't have to tell you about the judgment, the great flood of water that God is about to send on the world, do I? That's not what you wanted to know, is it? You know about it?"

"Yes," I said, "I know about it — and it is very sad."

"Very. But I'm concerned with a great rescue operation. It's very exciting!" Noah said. "As best I know how, I've followed all God's plans and commands. God's in the rescue operation, so I know everything will go just fine.

"I've told all the people how they too can escape God's judgment and have a place in this great rescue boat, if only they'd quit their sins. But they won't listen. They only mock or ignore what I say. It's going to be so terrible for them — so soon, too."

Neither of us spoke for a few minutes. I didn't like to look, but great tears were plopping on the ground — falling from old Noah's eyes.

Then — "So you'd like to look around, would you?"

"Please!" I said.

So we began to walk along the side of the great ark — flat bottom, flat top.

"Twice as high as our tall houses!" I said.

"About 30 cubits. Three floors. Three stories," Noah said.

"Thirty cubits, that's 45 feet," I said. "I've heard a cubit is from a man's elbow to the end of his middle finger."

"That's right," Noah said. "God gave me the measurement in cubits, and all the plans."

"Blueprints we call them," I said.

"They're not blue," Noah said, "but I know what you mean. God gave them to me anyway. Told me exactly what to do."

"This is a very long boat!" I said, as we walked along the ground beside it. "Four hundred and fifty feet — 150 yards! Oh, yes, I know you're going to say 300 cubits, but I know yards and feet. Four hundred and fifty feet — 150 yards long. I used to run the 150 yard race at school — won it once or twice. Long way for the length of a boat.

"And you've tarred the boat thickly."

"Yes, to keep the water out. 'Tar it inside and out,' God said. And I've done it," Noah told me.

"Good, hard wood," I said, knocking it.

Round the corner at the end of the great boat we went.

"Oh, this side is — what?"

"Fifty cubits," Noah said.

"Seventy-five feet," I said.

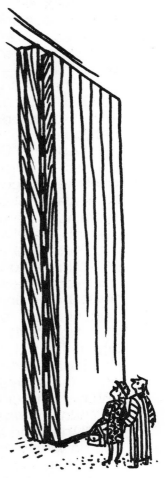

Round the next corner we walked and — "Oh, there's *the door* — in the other long side. May I look in?"

"Sure. Go ahead. Be quick though. Time's running out."

"The door goes all the way up. What a huge door!" I said. "How are you ever going to get it shut?"

"Not my job," said Noah. "God's! Not my job to open it either. God's job to shut and open the door. That's not my business, thank goodness."

"Three floors! Oh, smell the hay and apples and oranges and dried fruit! The outer walls tarred on the inside as well as the outside! — But all the rooms! — Oh, scores of rooms! — Made of woven reeds, the partitions are. — Air flows right through, and light! — Hay lofts over the stables! — Supplies just where needed! You have thought this out well, Noah."

"Altogether God's plan," Noah said. "Blueprint, did you call it?"

"Apples! Oranges! Dried apricots! Peaches! Grapes! Raisins! Nuts galore! Vegetables! — Oh, ah, what are you going to do for water, drinking water?"

"Water? Water? Did you say 'water?'" Noah was laughing. "There'll be plenty of water! And I've got a system. They'll all get water in their troughs."

"Won't the animals prey on each other?"

" 'Pray' did you say? I guess they may pray, but I don't know what they say." Noah gave me a queer look.

"Oh, I didn't mean that kind of pray, P-R-A-Y," I said. "I meant 'prey,' P-R-E-Y — eat each other."

"No, no, they won't do that here. Don't you know that animals forget their differences when there's danger about?"

"And you really expect the animals to come, Noah? You haven't got to catch them and drag them in?"

"Nope." Noah shook his head.

"And if and when they're all here, what on earth will you do with them?" I asked.

"They'll come. And I haven't got to catch them. God will tell the twos and the sevens and the birds and all the creepy-crawlies too."

"Oh, yes, it's mostly twos, isn't it? And sevens of sheep and goats and cattle. I just can't think how they'll know enough to come and get into this ark, this boat."

"Well, you know about birds and animals migrating, don't you? Same instinct. And maybe they'll all sleep quite a while. You've heard of creatures hibernating — going to sleep in the wintertime — haven't you? God has given His creatures all kinds of instincts. There's no problem," Noah said.

"So you aren't afraid of looking like a fool, Noah? What if nothing happens? People will laugh more."

"God has spoken," Noah said. "And forever God's Word is settled in heaven. Nothing surer. No, I'm not afraid of looking like a fool. I've been looking like one for

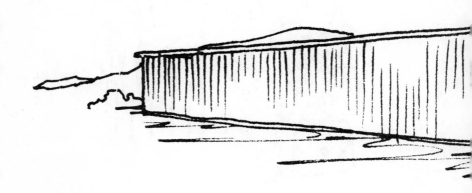

120 years. My boys, Shem, Ham, and Japheth, too. Not quite that long, but all their lives, though.

"No, no, I'm not afraid of looking like a fool. In less than a couple weeks' time, the whole world will know I'm right. Mind you, I'm sorry about it. But what can I do? I've told them. I can't drag them in. You'll see the animals come of their own accord, if you're around. But these people — no! I've done what I could. And here's the ark. You can see for yourself."

"It's a beauty, too," I said.

Noah was sadly shaking his head. "I've done all I could," he said.

"We have a saying," I said, trying to say something helpful. "You can lead a horse to the water, but you can't make him drink."

"That's just it," Noah said. "Just it."

Again, I didn't like to look, but big tears were running down Noah's cheeks, right down his beard.

"Everything's ready and about two weeks to go." There was a catch in his voice.

"It's like a countdown," I said.

Noah kept looking around and away to the horizon. I felt I was detaining him — taking up the time that was running out. But there were just one or two more

questions I wanted to ask him.

"About air, Noah," I said, trying to hurry up. "What are you going to do for air when you're all shut up in this ark with water all around everywhere?"

"Come," he said, "I'll show you."

Noah quickly walked a short distance away from the ark. I followed of course. Then he turned around to face the great structure. Pointing upwards towards the roof,

Noah said, "See the roof? Just below is an opening that runs all the way around the whole ark under the eaves. See how the roof extends to make eaves? The roof, extended like that, will shelter the opening a lot, and any rain blowing in won't be enough to matter. The opening doesn't seem very deep, looking at it from the ground here, but it's a cubit. You'd say — ?"

"Eighteen inches," I said.

"Well, that opening will let in all the air we need."

"Yes, but how can you have enough air from just eighteen — ?"

"Come now! Come on," Noah said, "don't you know anything about air conditioning and ventilation? Even fanner bees know about ventilation. They keep their hives air conditioned."

"We have air conditioners built in," I said.

"Spoilt! Everything done for you!" said Noah. "So you don't understand natural air conditioning? Tut, tut, tut!"

25

"Now come to think of it," I said, "I did feel a good draught of air when I peeped in the door on the ground floor there."

"You speak as if we ancients didn't know anything! We were skilled in music and all kinds of crafts before you were thought of — iron, bronze. . . . We were cattle farmers before you'd even seen a cow! And some of you must get out of your heads that things which happened before your times were non-events."

26

Noah looked as if he wished I'd go away. "You'd better get back to — "

"Yes, I'll go in a minute. Noah, pardon my asking you such a question as this, but I have a practical turn of mind and, judging by this magnificent structure, you have a practical turn of mind too: How are you going to clear out the litter? You say you'll be months in the ark."

"Oh, that's taken care of. Little trap doors in places. Didn't you see them? Sweep it out!"

"Oh, dear, why didn't I think of that?" I was feeling rather foolish by now.

"Oh, just one more thing," I said.

Noah really wanted me out of the way by now, I felt, but I had to ask him.

"Noah, my cat has an awful lot of kittens. They're sweet, but it's a job to know what to do with them all. And my rabbits and guinea pigs have a lot of babies. And as for the mice! So with all your animals, you're going to be overrun here in the ark before you know it."

"Oh, no! God has made arrangements. No births, no deaths in the ark. Every single thing is taken care of. Don't you worry. God has already whispered to the animals that are to come. They're on their way here now. Young ones, male and female. They'll be ready to start their families when the flood is over."

Noah spoke with great confidence about the flood. But not a soul believed him.

There wasn't a cloud in the sky. The sun had shone all day. It was getting dusk now.

"Stand back!" Noah shouted at me. He was getting excited.

"Oh, excuse me," he said. "Please stand back. They're coming!"

27

And so they were!

Noah and Shem and Ham and Japheth were on hand to direct if necessary.

The young animals came capering along, frolicking, happy as could be, and went straight into Noah's ark.

They found their niches. Food all ready. Cozy nests. Homes made-to-measure. What contented, cheery sounds came from those "homes" inside the ark!

People stood around and stared. But nobody went

into the ark. Oh, no! People laughed. Oh, how they laughed!

"Ha! ha! ha! You setting up a private zoo, Noah?"

Well, the creatures came and they came, and at the end of the week they were all in. Two and two. A young Mr. and Mrs. of every creature living on dry land. Sheep and goats and cattle came in sevens. God said they would.

At the end of the week God told Noah, "This is the day!" Noah had been waiting for it. He was ready. "In you go," God said. "In you go, and your wife and your sons and their wives."

They were all ready, so in they went — into the great ark.

How people laughed! This was the very funniest thing of all. Noah and his family carrying their suitcases, walking on board the ark as if they were going on a vacation.

"S'long, Noah!" people shouted.

All his family was mocked. But Noah got most of it because, as people said, *he* was the boss of the silly show.

"Come in! Won't you come in?" Noah was saying.

How they laughed, picturing themselves doing that — going into the ark with Noah.

"You'll be glad enough to come out again yourself in a week's time, Noah."

Just then the great door fell shut. That was a bit of a surprise. But they were all yelling, "S'long, Noah. Ha! ha! ha! See you next week! Ha! ha! ha!"

3

Water, Water Everywhere

Well, well, well — Noah and his family were the talk of the town.

"Heard the latest? Noah's shut himself in that great zoo of his!"

"What? You don't mean it!"

"Yes, I always said he was queer. The look in his eyes has always bothered me — faraway, far-seeing sort of look. Always made me feel uncomfortable!"

"So he's shut himself in it, has he? Gone quite off his rocker now, I guess. Of course he's a genius to have built that great thing. Fellows who've worked for him say he's very clever. But the scale's tipped now — he's right off, I guess. Where's his wife? How's she taking it? And the boys?"

"Oh, she's in there with him!"

"You don't say!"

"Yes, and the boys."

"What about their wives?"

"Oh, they've all gone in as well. Folks who saw them embark said they looked as if they were going on vacation!"

"Mind you, old Noah's got something about him to get his family to follow him like that. I'd never follow my old man on a crazy expedition."

"Nor me! Not on your life!"

"How do you account for all those animals going into the building?"

"Oh, well, you know as well as I do, animals will go for food. You could smell hay and stuff, apples — old Noah's got supplies of all kinds of goodies in there. Tons of food. And there's something about queer people like him — animals flock around them. They've got a way of talking to animals."

"Oh, give it a week, I say, and out they'll all come. I heard yesterday that Noah's family really went into the ark to get some quiet to mourn for old Methuselah.

"Oh, yes, what a great age he lived to — 969! He's the oldest person yet. Only fitting that the family should show respect for Noah's old grandfather."

"Yes, give 'em a week. They'll get tired of sitting mourning and moping in there."

"I hope there's no truth in his gloomy predictions of flood . . . deluge . . . judgment."

"Oh, come off it! None of that feeble-minded talk. I won't listen to it. Noah's just downright crazy, and that's that."

Actually, there were some who woke up and worried in the night.

"What if — ? He might be right! Noah *might* be right!"

But by morning, when the sun was up, they forgot their worries and laughed along with the rest.

Noah and his family had been in the ark for six days. Shut in. The door had stayed shut.

"I didn't think he'd shut the door! Fancy shutting the door!"

Nobody had peeped out anywhere. And nobody could peep in.

But let me tell you, inside it was so comfortable: plenty of good food — the best — and air conditioning. God's plan, don't forget!

And there they were — Noah, his wife, his sons Shem, Ham, and Japheth, and their wives, the animals in pairs, some in sevens, the birds, butterflies, and creepy-crawlies — all very comfortable, cozy, and

cared for. That was inside the ark. What was going on
outside now wasn't really their affair. Nothing to do with
them.

Things were going on of course. "Business as
usual" — out there.

"Nothing's going to happen! It's six days since old
Noah and company went into his crazy zoo and shut the
door."

Well, on the seventh morning people out there
woke up depressed. It was a gloomy day. No sunshine.
Great black clouds hung in the sky. It was depressing
and ominous. You could hear thunder in the distance.

And while people ate their breakfasts, great drops
of rain plopped everywhere.

"Oh, Noah may be right! Perhaps he is!" And those who could rushed to bang on the door of the ark.

"Noah, Noah, let us in! Do let us in! We're sorry we mocked you. Oh, please, please, let us in!"

From inside, if Noah could even have heard them, he'd have said, "I'm so sorry, folks. Now it's too late. I haven't got the power to open the door to let a single one of you in. God has shut the door, and I can't open it. I'm so sorry."

They banged and they clattered on that door.

At the same time as the rain and hail poured down, water surged up and gurgled from underground, from fountains and rivers and the ocean bed. And before long the ground was flooded over.

As the waters rose, the ark rose too. The waters lashed and surged, but the ark rolled along safely, and those inside were dry and warm.

As the boat rocked, some of the passengers were rocked to sleep. Oh, they were comfortable! And there was no way they could even see or hear what was going on outside. The ark was waterproof and soundproof — almost.

The birds sang their best songs. Every creature in that great ark felt so safe and contented. You should have heard the happy murmur, the purrs and grunts and little yelps of delight, even a happy "heehaw" from the donkeys.

Inside, you could smell the apples and oranges and hay — and the animals.

Outside — oh, I hate to tell you what was going on outside the ark. As the waters surged and rose, people climbed onto their roofs — then to the tallest trees, clutching their most precious belongings. People tried to rush to higher ground, to mountains — but the waters engulfed them before they got very far. Oh, it was terrible. Soon everything that had lived on dry land was drowned — dead.

37

For forty days water poured down from the sky and surged and spewed up from underground.

Soon the whole earth was covered with one vast ocean — as it had been before God made the dry land appear at Creation.

For forty days the water poured and spewed and gushed and surged like that. Forty days nonstop.

Then the rain stopped. And the gushing stopped. And for 150 days — five months — the water stayed just like that. Oh, the water was deep! The highest mountains were covered, and the water was deep even over the tops of the mountains.

The Bible tells us that God gave special thought and care to Noah and all who were with him in the ark — people and animals.

The ark was still floating, gently now. All the storm had passed. The sun shone in through the slats in the roof. (Did I tell you about the slats in the roof?) Noah had drawn the covering skins off the slats when the rain stopped, and the sunshine pouring in through the openings was very cheery.

After five months' cruising — with the very nicest food to eat and no sickness, worries, rent, or taxes, and a guaranteed safe landing — Noah and his family could somehow feel, as the ark floated, that the waters were draining away.

At the end of another five months, they found that they weren't floating any longer. They had come to a standstill.

The ark wobbled a bit. They didn't know where they

were of course. And it was something for that huge craft to get settled on really flat ground. What a tragedy if a bit of the structure got caught up on a mountain peak and toppled the whole thing over! As if that could happen when God was in control!

But can't you hear Mrs. Noah: "Noah, I'm getting so worried. I'm ashamed, for I know I shouldn't — but what if our ark doesn't settle on flat ground? We could topple over and be crushed to death after all."

"Now, my dear, you've been a brave old girl," Noah said. "Where's your faith gone? We're almost at the end of it. Don't lose heart now."

"I'll try not to," Mrs. Noah said. "But I've been noticing little bumps — not all little either — as if the ground wasn't flat. Be awful if we were to tip."

If Mrs. Noah could have seen where they were! They were landing in a mountain range in Turkey — miles from home.

And the mountains! Oh, it was a good thing they couldn't see — for the moment. They couldn't have done anything if they could have seen, and they might have panicked!

But God had everything in hand, and He brought that ark to rest in a beautiful spot in the mountains of Ararat. A perfect landing — no more wobbles. Those inside couldn't tell yet where they were, but Mrs. Noah felt safe again.

Noah said, "Well, we've stopped floating. If we're on high ground, then water will still be covering the plains and the valleys. But there's no way I can tell."

Seven days later — a week later — he said, "I know. . . ."

4

Off to a New Start

"I know," Noah said. "I know — I'll open the window a tiny bit and let a raven and a dove fly out. I'll see what happens."

So Noah opened the little window in the roof of the great ark and out flew the raven and the dove.

"We've been landed here seven days now," Noah said. "Can't tell if we're up or down — up on a mountain or down in the valley. If we're up, then the flood water will still be covering the plains and it will be deep in the valleys.

"Anyway, God hasn't opened the door yet to let us out. And I certainly can't open it. That's God's job. He shut it. He'll open it. But I'd like to know where we are.

"God has kept us all safe, the eight of us, and all the animals. Plenty to eat, good health, happiness. Now, of course, we'd all like to get out. But we'll be told when."

Before nightfall, Noah saw that the dove was back, perched on the ark roof by the window, asking to be let in again. (The raven could keep flying backwards and forwards until the water dried up — it was a big, strong bird — but the dove was a gentle little thing.)

Noah let the dove in through the opening in the roof.

"Ah, must be a lot of water about still," Noah said. "The dove hasn't found anywhere to rest."

Even so, it couldn't be too long now before they'd all be able to go out. And the door hadn't given a hint of opening yet. The door, after all, was God's business.

At the end of the next week, Noah opened the window again and let the dove fly out once more.

The dove stayed away longer than she had before. Was she coming back?

Oh, there — there she was, perched beside the window, waiting to be let back into the ark.

Noah saw her and went to let her in. Oh, what was she holding in her beak? What was it?

"Well, well," Noah said, as he put out his hand to take the dove in, "just look here. A leaf! Let me see. What kind of leaf? It's a new little olive leaf. Now that shows that seedlings have begun to grow again. The water must be nearly gone. All gone in places."

You should have heard the thanksgiving that went on in the ark that evening. The dove had plucked off an olive leaf and brought it home! (Did you know that a dove with a little olive branch in its beak is a symbol of peace, right to this very day? I'm sure you've seen a picture of it.)

Well, Noah waited seven more days — another week. And then he let the dove out again.

And although Noah kept waiting for her to perch again beside the window on the roof, she didn't come back.

Now though I'm sure Noah was fond of the dove and liked having her around in the ark — she was a gentle little thing, that dove — even so, he wasn't sorry that she didn't come back.

"Ah," said Noah, "it won't be long now. The dove has found a nice place to live — somewhere she likes

better than the ark. Any day now we'll be out there too!"

They were all getting very excited. What would it be like?

In just another seven days God said, "Noah, this is the day!"

God opened the door, and the animals filed out — hopping, skipping, jumping. The birds flew past, and the butterflies, and the bees.

You should have seen those animals skipping and frolicking into a bright new world — all fresh and green. Grass and flowers, all clean and new and beautiful, rather like the world was right at the beginning when God put Adam and Eve into Eden. Of course, the flood wiped out any landmark that might have been Eden.

But here was the lovely new world. The world after the Flood.

"Multiply! There's plenty of room for you," God told the birds and animals, as they flew and skipped away to make their lovely homes and have their families. "Multiply! Fill the earth again!"

Now Noah and his family were so thankful to God, so full of praise, there was only one way they could show it, and that was by offering a sacrifice. This is what Noah did, there and then. (Remember there were seven of some animals, like sheep and goats?)

God understood that Noah and his family were trying to say "Thank You." God accepted their gratitude and worship.

"Noah," God said, "from now on I'm going to allow you to eat meat as well as fruits and vegetables." So Noah and his family did, and they enjoyed "roasts" just as much as anybody.

God told Noah several other things — about life being sacred and how Noah was to rule this lovely new world.

Then God said, "Never again, Noah!" God said, "Never again!"

Noah looked up from his sacrificing.

"No," God said, "I will never, never do it again! I will never destroy the whole world with a flood again.

"Man is just man . . . full of evil, wicked intentions . . . simply can't go straight. Yet, while the earth remains, there will always be seedtime and harvest, always summer and winter, always cold and heat, always day and night.

"Look up, Noah," God said. "I want you to look. What do you see in the sky?" (What ever was it?)

It was a beautiful, perfect rainbow.

"Noah, whenever there's been rain and you see My bow in the sky, you're to remember My promise: 'So long as the earth remains, there will always be seedtime and harvest, summer and winter, day and night.'

"And, Noah, as you look at the rainbow, it is My promise to you that I will never ever destroy the whole world with a flood again."

And God's promise still holds good! Whenever you see a rainbow in the sky, take a good look at all its lovely colors and say to yourself, "God is remembering His promise."

I saw a rainbow yesterday, and I remembered that God was keeping His promise. And I was glad!

46

5

Any Day Now!

Now I've got something special to tell you about the ark. Do you know that one of these days you could wake up in the morning and hear on your radio or read in your newspaper that the ark of Noah has been found? You could even see pictures of it on your television screen! Headlines: BIBLE PROVED RIGHT — NOAH'S ARK FOUND.

Let me tell you about it — and we just don't know which day the secret could be out.

Way up in the mountains in the country of Turkey, close to the Russian border, is Mount Ararat. It stands there high — 17,000 feet high — towering above the other mountains around it.

The top of Mount Ararat is crowned with a great thick icecap. In fact, its summit is covered by a huge glacier which moves very, very slowly.

Now, in a kind of cove, a big sheltered nook, on that mountain, there's thick ice too — another glacier. But the ice that covers that cove can't move — it's stuck.

Although I say "nook," it's not a small place. It's 650 feet long and 150 feet wide. (Do you want it in cubits? Well, 433 cubits long, 100 cubits wide.) Some cove! — 650 feet by 150 feet wide. That cove could hold the ark just nicely.

Well, it's said that that is the spot where "the secret" lies in the deep ice of the trapped glacier.

The Bible, of course, tells us how God instructed Noah to build the ark of gopher wood, a sort of cyprus wood — hard, unrottable wood. Three stories the ark was to be, with many rooms for all the animals. And the ark was to be coated with a waterproof substance. And it was!

Then when the flood was over, the ark came to rest — landed, grounded, settled — on the mountains of Ararat.

Well, ever since the ark landed there on Mount Ararat, down through the ages and right till now, there have been reports of individuals who've seen the stranded ark.

There's been talk of hundreds of rooms . . . of walking in rooms, big and little, large and small, that happened to be exposed, jutting out of the ice at the time . . . of taking measurements . . . and getting little bits of the reddish-black wood — hand-tooled — that's coated with stuff like shellac.

Actually, not too long ago a fairly large piece of this wood was picked up and taken to a university science laboratory to be tested for age. (That's called the carbon test.) And the report came back: "This wood is of great antiquity. Could be 5,000 years old." (Not far out for the ark!)

At different times through the ages and even now "the secret" has been more or less visible, depending on the season — the weather sometimes being a little milder. When the temperature has risen a bit, some of the ice has melted a little and "the secret," or parts of "the secret," could be seen.

Then, at other times, piles of snow from terrible blizzards and hail and thicker ice, as well as landslides of rocks and debris, have hidden "the secret" altogether. That's how "the secret" lies just now — hidden.

I have a friend who is a professor of archaeology, and he says, "It seems as if God has the ark in His deep-freeze, and when He's ready He'll bring it out." That will be the day!

Won't it be a surprising day for those who, like the people in Noah's day, haven't taken the ark story seriously?

If ever the time comes when "the secret" is out, I'll be on the phone to my travel agent.

"Will you please book me on the first possible plane for Mount Ararat?"

"Certainly. Oh, is that Mrs. G.?"

"Yes!"

"Well, how about tomorrow?"

"Nothing sooner?"

"All booked I'm afraid. Oh, but wait a minute, I think I could squeeze you on a plane tonight."

"Yes, that would be great."

And I'd rush off to pack my anorak and climbing boots. . . .

"Oh, what else do I need? . . . Ah, yes. . . ." And away I'd go.

It would be exciting!

Of course, we don't know if this will ever happen. But we do know that when Jesus was on earth, preaching and healing and loving people, He talked about Noah and the ark — repentance and judgment.

"Don't let the Judgment (and He didn't mean a flood) overtake you unawares," He said. "Watch and be ready! I am coming again — suddenly.

"It will be too late then to change your plans — just as it was too late for people to get into the ark when the flood was upon them. Be ready *now!*" Jesus said.

Now you and I don't have to be worried, because we know that right now we can be ready — forgiven right now. And when the end of the world comes for you and me, away we'll go into God's bright new world to be with Him forever in heaven. Won't that be the day?

That's what God's plan is all about.

51

52

6

Noah's "Accident"

When Noah and his family stepped out of the ark, the world was back to square one. Bright, beautiful, and clean once more.

All the wickedness and filth had been wiped out — washed away — by the Flood. Noah and his wife and their sons, Shem, Ham, and Japheth, along with their wives, were the only people in the world. Eight of them. Stalwarts for God they'd been in the days before the Flood while they built the ark, no matter how much ridicule came their way. And now they had the world to themselves — and God.

Some world it would be now, with only these good people in it. So you would think. But just let me whisper in your ear: "Satan was not drowned in the Flood and. . . ."

But just now everything looked so lovely. God said to Noah and his sons, "Multiply! Fill the earth!" And they began to.

No more fear ever of such a flood again. The rainbow now and then would remind them of God's promise, as it does us.

God gave some fundamental instructions about the new world: human life was to be sacred . . . animals and birds would have a certain fear of people . . . man was lord of creation.

They were off to a new start. Exciting!

And wasn't Mrs. Noah thankful to get her feet on solid ground once more?

"A year's cruise may be all right for some people, but give me terra firma and me own kitchen!" I can just hear her.

Noah's grandchildren began to arrive. Shem, Ham, and Japheth all had their fair share of little girls and boys. And of course they were all cousins. They played together — no one else to play with. They had the world to themselves, the Noah tribe.

And old Noah was the chief — God's great friend. I called him "old" because when he stepped out of the ark after the Flood he was 601 years old. Of course, you'll remember I told you once that in those days people lived many, many years without getting worn out or sick or weak. So at 601 Noah was still going strong. And he was to live 350 years more.

Now with all the good, fertile land around and so few people about, you'd expect the Noah tribe to get down to farming and sheep and cattle-rearing. They did, and made a great job of it.

Most farmers have a specialty, something they're awfully good at growing, like corn or potatoes or beans — something that's just their "cup of tea." Noah had a specialty, too. It was growing grapes. He just had a knack with grapes.

Grapes had been around since the Garden of Eden days, but nobody had ever gone in for growing them on a large scale. Mind you, that's surprising, because they are so delicious. Noah thought so and grew a lot. He was an absolute expert at growing grapes.

Now there's a story in the Bible about Noah's grapes, and it's the only story we're told about Noah's long life after the Flood. The only story about him in all those 350 years, which is rather strange in a way.

Noah was like a king. He made laws, rules for people to live by. And he'd always been God's special friend.

"Build the ark!" God had told him. "You're in charge of the great rescue operation during the deluge." And God had given him the blueprints. It was an engineering feat that astonishes us today.

And there must have been many other things that happened to a man like Noah in the 350 years that he lived after the Flood. . . . But we're only told the story about his growing grapes.

Mind you, it isn't a nice story.

I found it in the Bible when I was a little girl. I'd been

told about Noah and the ark, but not about Noah and the grapes.

Nobody had told me about it or explained it to me, so I said, "Why?" and I asked somebody about it.

"Oh, it isn't a nice story, dear."

"But it's in the Bible!" I said.

So in case you feel the same way I did, I'm going to haul the skeleton out of the cupboard and tell you the story. Then you'll know and understand about it. It's better to look the facts squarely in the face, isn't it?

The fact of the matter is that Noah got drunk.

"No! Not Noah!"

Yes, Noah.

Now I'm not blaming him — God didn't. Noah was terribly upset about it. But God didn't blame him. You see, it was an accident.

But there were those who got into terrible trouble for being vulgar and making a mock of Noah while he was drunk.

I guess it happened like this.

People had eaten grapes before, but no one had ever grown such a quantity of grapes before. Noah's vines in his new vineyard produced so many luscious grapes that he just couldn't eat them all — even though he gave bunches away to the rest of his tribe.

When you get a bumper crop of fruit, you think of all kinds of ways of using that fruit, don't you? Well, Noah did — with the Mrs. helping.

They squeezed the grapes down and made delicious grape juice and drank it. But they couldn't get it all used up daily, and they had no refrigerator or freezer.

Tomorrow's ripe grapes were gathered before yesterday's juice was used up. Fresh juice was being squeezed before the last lot was all drunk. So some was left neglected — standing in a jar in the corner of the tent.

Nobody knew how long that juice stood there in the jar in the corner.

Then some more luscious grapes were brought in from the vineyard.

"Come on, we must squeeze them down," Noah said.

"No more jars," said his wife.

Noah looked around. "What about that big one in the corner? Nothing in it, is there?"

Mrs. Noah went to look. "Oh, there's stale juice in it," she said.

"I'll throw that out," Noah said. "Then we can use the jar. Here, give it to me.

"Oh, the smell of it! I like the smell. What does it taste like? . . . Tastes good! . . . (Noah smacked his lips.)

"Here, find me a smaller pitcher. I'll keep it — come back to it. Let's use this big jar for the fresh juice that we're going to squeeze now."

So they did. . . .

Later, Noah was in the tent all by himself, tidying things up a bit. "Ah, yes, this pitcher of stale juice," he said to himself as he came across it. "Smells interesting . . . tastes different! I can just do with a little drink right now. . . . (Noah smacked his lips.) Ah, lovely!"

Noah was thirsty. He didn't stop at a little drink. . . . "To think I nearly threw this stuff out. . . ."

Wow! It threw Noah. It knocked Noah right out. He began to act queerly — not himself at all. He lashed around . . . pulled off his clothes . . . made the oddest noises. . . .

Noah's son Ham and, it seems, Ham's son Canaan, passing by, looked into Noah's tent to see what on earth was going on. And what they saw and heard tickled them to death. How those two laughed!

The great Noah, the boss who always told them what to do, the great man who had direct contact with God — the great Noah was sprawled out on the floor of his tent, fast asleep, dead drunk, and naked.

Oh, how Ham and Canaan laughed to see Noah in this awful state. They came rolling and rollicking and laughing out of old Noah's tent. Evil, mocking laughter.

"Ha! ha! ha! You should see — it's so funny, Shem."

"See what?" Shem asked. "What's the matter with you?"

"Oh, dad's in a state. Oh, it's so funny to see the good and great like that. Does something for you, it does. Makes me feel ten feet tall. Ha! ha! ha! It's so funny."

Bit by bit the description came out.

"What do you mean? Is dad dying?" Japheth had joined the noisy group.

"No, there's nothing dying about him! Ha! ha! Come and see. Ha! ha! ha! Looks like he's been drinking old grape juice. There's an empty pitcher on the floor and a smell of stale juice."

Shem and Japheth were furious to hear their wonderful father being mocked by their brother Ham and that vulgar whippersnapper, their nephew Canaan.

"If father is lying on his tent floor in that state, we must do something quickly," Shem said. "We must cover him. Where's my cloak?"

"Here, Japheth, you take this corner. Hold it shoulder high with your left hand, and I'll hold this corner shoulder high with my right hand. Like so. And we'll drag the cloak as we walk backwards into dad's tent. We'll not look at him. We'll drop the cloak on him to cover him up."

They did just that. At least *they* wouldn't gaze on their revered old father in this predicament.

Shem and Japheth had more to say to Ham and Canaan outside. They were terribly angry.

"Don't be so squeamish and delicate about it," Ham said. "Can't you see the funny side of this? It's terribly funny. Dad's been telling us what to do all our lives; now look at him. It's fun to laugh at him when he can't even tell us off."

"What kind of humor have you got, Ham, to think that obscene things are funny? Don't teach your boy to be so disgusting. It's up to us to cover dad and lessen his shame," Shem said. (Actually, that boy Canaan must have been worse than his dad.)

Later on old Noah came to. He felt very queer. Where was he? What had been happening? Oh, he'd been asleep a long time. . . . He could still taste it — what was it?

"Oh, yes, that stale grape juice . . . must have put me to sleep . . . my head feels funny. . . ."

Then he began to put two and two together. His clothes — had he pulled off his clothes? He went hot and cold at the thought. People had looked at him . . . seen him as he'd lain there, not knowing what he was doing.

Then this cloak. . . . Someone had tried to preserve his dignity, someone had cared. . . . "Oh, bless him! Bless them!

"It's Shem's cloak. Did Shem put it there? Oh, Shem must have seen me, naked. How low I've been brought. . . ."

Minutes later, Noah was dressed and out of his tent, upset, ashamed.

He called for his sons and demanded to know what had happened.

"I should have thrown that juice out, boys — it's brought me so low in your eyes."

Ham and son looked sheepish now. They had nothing to say. Shem and Japheth didn't want to talk. No one was prepared to say much. But Noah was asking questions, demanding answers.

"How did you find out?"

The story came out, bit by bit. The whole story. (You can't be vague with a man like Noah, can you now? He was bound to get to the bottom of things when he was in his right mind. He did.)

"Shem — Japheth," the old man said, "I am grateful to you. You did a very kind and delicate thing in those nasty circumstances. I am grateful."

Noah gave Shem and Japheth a magnificent blessing from God. He predicted good for Shem and Japheth.

But for Ham and Canaan, Noah predicted trouble. "You will be a servant of servants — the lowest of slaves — to your brothers," Noah said.

Ham and Canaan didn't like that. But Noah's prophecy came true. The Canaanites, who were Canaan's descendants, did become the servants of the

Israelites, who were Shem's descendants. But that's another story.

Ham and his tribe didn't take Noah's curse lying down. Oh, no! "Who said we'd be servants?" they said. "We won't be servants! We'll show 'em! We'll be the greatest. Come on, we'll, we'll — —." Just wait till you hear what they did.

7

Building Without a Permit

Noah's "accident" showed what his sons were really like. Shem and Japheth were decent people — but Ham! Ham and his son Canaan were downright vulgar.

Noah made his predictions — doled out blessings and a curse. Blessings for Shem and Japheth; the very opposite for Ham and Canaan: "Slaves, the lowest of slaves, you'll be to your brothers, and it will go on and on, right through your family for all time," Noah told Canaan.

Grandson Canaan was particularly mentioned because he was particularly vulgar. Actually, later Canaan's family started up the most horrible heathen religion and taught people abominable practices. And God punished them. He took their country away from them and gave it to the Israelites, who were, of course, the sons of Shem.

But right now, Noah's words must have rankled. Rebellion must have smoldered in Ham and his descendants.

"Slaves?" they said. "Slaves? Not us! We'll rule instead!"

And one of Ham's family — years later — Nimrod, showed great leadership along this line.

He was some boy, that Nimrod. He was a fantastic hunter. And a great ambition had grown in his mind: "I'll get hordes of people together," he said. "God said, 'Spread out,' did He? Bah! Let's get masses of people together, I say, and *I'll* be the boss."

Nimrod's very name means "Let's rebel! — revolt!" He was full of defiance; he strutted and boasted — before the Lord even! Under God's very nose.

Nimrod rallied his tribe, which was very large indeed by now, and he influenced his second cousins and his nth cousins. (Most of Shem's lot wouldn't listen to Nimrod. They'd gone off by themselves anyway, and old Noah was with them.)

God had said: "Multiply! Spread out! Fill the earth!" These people said: "Oh, no, not us! We'll stay together in one big city and make a name for ourselves. The more we are together, the merrier we shall be — and the stronger we shall be. No, no, we won't spread out. We'll built a huge city and a tower — up, and up, and up — right up to heaven. If there's enough of us, and we keep close together . . . well, unity is strength!"

Now with the ark still there on Mount Ararat for everyone to see if they looked, you'd think that people would be a little bit careful.

Although God had said, "I won't destroy the world with a flood again," He hadn't said that people could do just what they liked, live any old way, never give Him a thought. No, no, God had not said that.

Well, you'd think that the Flood had been enough of a warning, and the ark enough of a reminder. But listen!

This gathering took place on the lovely plain between the rivers Tigris and Euphrates. The spokesman was Nimrod.

Nimrod was really in league with Satan by now. How the people looked up to Nimrod! They practically worshiped him, as well as idols of all kinds — birds, animals, reptiles. You can worship almost anything once you turn your back on God. These people did.

Well, Nimrod, the spokesman, began in a booming voice: "God has told us to spread out. We won't! Let's stick together in one big, enormous city. (Cheers.)

"Let's build the largest city that ever we can. (Cheers, cheers.) And let's build the biggest, highest tower that ever was. (Cheers, cheers.) And let's make the top of it reach right up to heaven, where God is supposed to be." (Cheers.)

The crowd went mad. . . .

They chose the site carefully on the great, beautiful plain between the rivers. They organized . . . drew up plans . . . engaged architects and draftsmen . . . ordered materials . . . hired workers.

They needed hundreds and hundreds of workers, of course. Everything had to be done by hand. No cranes or bulldozers then. Imagine the number of workers that had to be engaged to build a great city and a tower, the biggest, most gigantic tower that ever was. There just had to be hundreds and hundreds of workers.

Now round about on this great plain, but farther away, people had already built towers. These towers were called ziggurats.

A ramp, built on the outside wall of the ziggurat, went round and round, and up and up. No elevators, no escalators! But there were stairs inside the tower.

The idea was that you built a tower as high as you

could afford, or as high as you dared to go. And right on the very top you made a temple to your god. (They'd invented all kinds of gods by now. Nimrod was a god himself, almost.)

The higher the better, of course, because the higher your ziggurat the more prestige your city had.

This lot, Ham's descendants, with Nimrod in charge, were a bold lot. They were going to have a higher tower than anybody else — all the difference between a mountain and little mole heaps.

So they bustled about in a very businesslike, lordly manner. Everything must be ready for the job — tools, bricks, tar, and workers.

Workers began to move into the plain, keeping outside the boundary lines of the proposed city, of course. The workers arrived with their families and tents and sheep and goats.

Sheep and goats would provide some food — milk and meat — and they'd cultivate garden plots beside their tents to give them corn and vegetables. Of course, they must eat!

The plain was black with tents and goats and sheep, and workers.

And this tremendous tower and city would take years to build, however much the workers hurried or however hard they worked.

Bricks were ordered. Piles of bricks arrived. Bricks had to be made on the spot too. Just how many bricks would these people need? Kilns had to be made to fire the bricks, and at night you could see red-hot kilns glowing in the dark across the plain.

They had meetings — planning meetings.

"Now we must have good stuff to fix the bricks together, something that will last. We can't have things falling apart — disintegrating. Sometimes the Euphrates River overflows and floods the plain; we must use something that won't rot."

"Ah, bitumen! That's what old Noah used for the ark, didn't he? Bitumen — pitch, tar — that's the stuff. It's waterproof. We'll use it to stick the bricks together."

"And our tower will be so high that if we had a flood like that one — Noah's — the water would never reach to the top of *our* tower. *Our* tower will be higher than the highest mountain."

My, it was some enterprise! You should have seen President Nimrod . . . chairman . . . vice-chairman . . . corporation members . . . committee members.

Then there were the architects and the draftsmen mapping out the blueprints. The master masons and the carpenters and the foremen, and all the Toms, Dicks, and Harrys doing the actual job — digging the foundations, making the bricks, firing the bricks and laying the bricks, sealing them with tar.

"Come on! This is going to be the greatest!"

They made an enormous broad bottom for their tower. It had to have a huge base to support the height they expected to attain.

And at the same time as the tower, the huge city they had planned was being built, too.

Just everybody was at it, and everybody was saying, "Spread out? Who said 'Spread out'? No, we don't want to spread out. We *won't* spread out! We want to stay together. Unity is strength! If there's any trouble, there's a lot of us and we are powerful. We'll get up to heaven! See if we don't."

God heard every word of their big boast. He wasn't pleased, but He let them get on with it. And they were getting on with it. Look how high the tower was already — almost touching the clouds.

They held parties and gloated. Things were going so well for the tower and the city.

"Nothing will stop us," they boasted. "We'll stick together. We'll get up to heaven!"

Their blasphemy was terrible to listen to. They looked powerful and glorious.

74

God saw and heard. (God misses nothing, of course.) God didn't like what He saw and heard. (You didn't expect He would, did you?)

"This nonsense has got to stop," God said. And He didn't look for a messenger to take His message either. This was no time for a messenger. Who'd listen to a messenger?

There was noise and clangor and clatter down there on the plain. They were busy. They held hectic, rousing meetings. People got worked up. Nimrod was in charge, and he had them all going his way.

They all spoke the same language; they understood each other; they were comrades in rebellion. Mind you, some were just follow-the-leader types. But they were in rebellion against God whether they knew it or not. Nimrod was their leader, and he knew.

God looked and listened. And He began to laugh at their great hollow boasts and their puny might. He didn't say anything. He just made something happen that was really funny.

God doled out new languages — just like that!

Everybody was busy when it happened. And from that moment onwards, the words they were saying, which seemed perfectly good words to the speaker, didn't mean a thing to the people who were being spoken to.

They began to stare at each other blankly, then to quarrel. And although the quarreling words meant nothing to them now, the tone of voice did, of course. The result was irritation, anger, and frustration.

Well, you've just no idea how confused those people got. They couldn't get on at all. The work just had to stop, because nobody knew what anybody else was saying.

Fortunately, children could understand their parents; so little families kept together all right. But there weren't enough people speaking any one language to carry on an enterprise of that size and nature — building a great city and the most enormous tower that ever was.

Now the people didn't want to stay together. They looked blankly into each other's faces. They just couldn't stand each other!

No one thought of writing grammar books and embarking on the study of foreign languages. No, each family group got by itself — as far away from the others

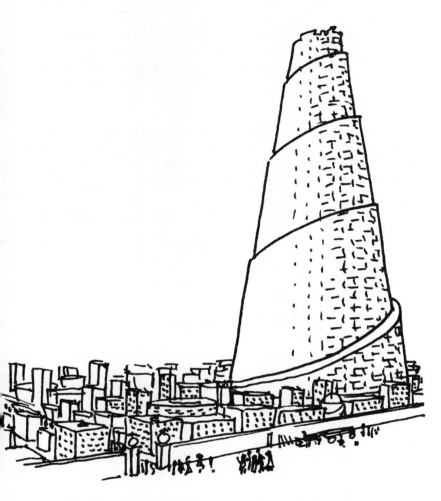

as possible. They spread out all right. Far and wide.
They were glad to!
So the tower was left standing — half-built.

The name of the tower was Babel, which means "Confusion." The name of the city was Babylon.

Nimrod and his family stayed around Babylon, finished building the city themselves, and made it famous in the Bible for idol worship. But the tower was never finished.

For a while after all this happened, God waited for another man whom He could trust to carry out His great plan. Oh, no, God hadn't forgotten His plan! He's just never in a hurry. But He had to wait a long time for His next man.

He got him at last, and his name was — but that's another story!

Be sure to read about the man God chose to carry out His plan, in Mrs. G.'s next book in the series, Come, Meet Abraham, the Pioneer.